ADVENTURE PARK

RAINFOREST RIOT

By Cavan Scott • Illustrated by Abby Ryder

Titles in the Adventure Park set

Dinosaur Danger

Monster Mayhem

Pirate Peril

Candy Crisis

Cosmic Chaos

Rainforest Riot

Medieval Madness

Pyramid Panic

Badger Publishing Limited,
Oldmedow Road, Hardwick Industrial Estate,
King's Lynn PE30 4JJ

Telephone: 01438 791037
www.badgerlearning.co.uk

2 4 6 8 10 9 7 5 3 1

Rainforest Riot ISBN 978-1-78464-343-0

Publisher: Susan Ross
Senior Editor: Danny Pearson
Editorial Coordinator: Claire Morgan
Illustration: Abby Ryder
Designer: Bigtop Design

Meet Emily. Her grandfather owns Adventure Park. It's the best theme park in the world!

Meet Jacob. He's Emily's best friend.

Meet Frank. He's Emily's pet hamster.

Together, they test Adventure Park's new rides.

Some of the rides are magical. Some of the rides are scary. Some of the rides are dangerous. But ALL of the rides are exciting!

Join Emily, Jacob and Frank on the adventure of a lifetime.

Contents

Cast of Characters

carriage – a container with wheels used to carry people from one place to another.

safari – a journey to see animals in the wild.

mane – the long hair around a lion's head.

totem pole – a large post, made from a tree, covered with carved images.

Tree Terror

"Climb faster!" Emily shouted.

"I'm going as fast as I can!" Jacob called back.

The jungle was hot. Too hot. Emily's palms were sweating. If she slipped and fell she would be in real trouble.

At the bottom of the tree, the monster clawed at the trunk.

Jacob hung onto a branch above her. "So, got any bright ideas?" he asked.

Emily shook her head. Usually she was the one who came up with a plan. Usually she was the one who saved the day.

This time was different.

This time she didn't have a clue what to do.

But wait a minute! We've jumped to the middle of the story.

What are Jacob and Emily doing in a jungle? And where's Frank, Emily's pet hamster?

Well, it all started when Albert Sparkle-Trousers bounced up to see them on a bright yellow space hopper.

Albert was Emily's grandfather and the owner of Adventure Park.

He was also really bad at bouncing.

WHAM!

Albert landed headfirst in a rubbish bin.

Jacob ran over and pulled him out.

"Thank you, young man," Albert said.

"No problem," said Jacob, rubbing his hands together.

He was wearing a long scarf. "All that bouncing must keep you warm. It's really chilly today."

"I never feel the cold," Albert said. "Not when I'm wearing my hat."

He tapped the safari helmet on his head.

"There's no time to lose," Albert said, rushing over to a large sign. "You need to test my new ride!"

Frank the hamster ran up to Emily's shoulder and looked at the sign.

RAINFOREST RIOT

"Rainforest Riot," he read. "What is it?"

"Adventure Park's very own safari!" Albert said excitedly.

Emily peeked around the sign. She couldn't believe what she saw.

A rainforest had appeared in the middle of the Park.

RAINFOREST
RIOT

On Safari!

Tall trees stretched high into the sky.

"This is crazy!" Emily said. "Since when did we have a jungle?"

"I planted it last Tuesday," Albert told her. "I got some seeds from the garden centre. I think they were a bit magic."

Albert hurried them into a small carriage. "This will drive you through the jungle," he said. "You'll see all kinds of wild animals."

Frank's whiskers twitched. "What kinds of wild animals?"

"Oh, lions and tigers!" said Albert. He slammed the carriage's door shut. "Nothing to worry about!"

"There's always *something* to worry about on one of your rides!" Frank said, but the carriage was already moving.

Albert waved them goodbye. "Just watch out for the hamster-eating spiders!" he shouted after them.

"The what?" Frank cried out.

"He's teasing you!" laughed Emily. "There's no such thing."

"Probably," Jacob added with a smile.

They passed one animal after another.

Giraffes ate the leaves from the trees. Hippos dozed on muddy banks. Birds swooped through the sky.

"This is amazing!" Emily said.

"And much hotter!" said Jacob.

"Look," said Emily, pointing ahead. "Is that a lion?"

"A l-l-l-lion?" gulped Frank.

She was right. A lion was running towards them. It was huge, with a bushy mane. It had sharp claws and even sharper teeth.

"It's going to eat us!" Frank squeaked. "Help!"

The King of the Beasts

The lion ran closer.

"I don't want to be a lion's lunch!" Frank wailed.

Emily frowned. "I don't think it wants to eat us," she said. "It just looks scared!"

Jacob nodded. "You're right. I think it's being chased!"

"But what chases a lion?" Frank asked.

"That!" said Emily, pointing past the lion.

Behind it, a massive creature jumped out of the trees.

It was the size of an elephant with jagged teeth, giant ears and a long, winding tail.

"But that's impossible!" said Jacob.

It was a mouse. The biggest mouse in the world.

The lion ran straight past them and the giant mouse followed. With a flick of its tail, it knocked the carriage over.

Emily, Jacob and Frank tumbled out.

By the time they looked up, both the lion and mouse were gone.

"How did a mouse get so big?" asked Frank.

"And fierce!" Jacob added.

Emily heard something.

She ran over to a thick tree trunk and peeked around. "It's not just the mice that are big," she said.

Jacob and Frank joined her. On the other side of the tree, a gorilla was fighting a giant ladybird!

"What's doing this?" Emily whispered.

"Me!" a voice boomed.

The friends spun around.

Behind them stood a terrifying Totem Pole!

"What are you doing in my jungle?" the Totem Pole snarled.

"It's not your jungle," Emily said. "It belongs to my grandfather!"

"Silence!" the Totem Pole shouted. "This jungle is too noisy. All those nasty animals roaring and screeching. I can't get to sleep for all the noise!"

"Is that's why you've turned all those small animals and bugs into monsters?" Jacob asked. "You want all the animals to fight and scare each other away from the jungle!"

"That's just mean!" added Frank.

"Mean?" shouted the Totem Pole. **"I'll show you mean!"**

A beam of light shot from the Totem Pole's eyes.

It hit Frank, knocking him from Emily's shoulder.

"Frank!" Emily cried, but something weird was happening.

Frank was growing. He got bigger and bigger and bigger.

Soon he was twice the size of Emily and Jacob.

Frank glared down at them with red eyes. His fur looked like the bristles of a brush, and his teeth were razor-sharp.

"Frank?" Jacob said. "Are you OK, buddy?"

Frank didn't answer. Instead, he opened his mouth and roared!

CHAPTER 5 Run!

Jacob grabbed Emily's hand and ran.

"What's happened to Frank?" he asked.

"The Totem Pole has turned him into a monster!" Emily said. "Quick! Climb this tree!"

They scrambled up the tree trunk.

Beneath them, Frank clawed at the bark.

"That serves you right!" the Totem Pole yelled up at them. "Coming into my jungle and making all this noise!"

Jacob reached the top of the tree.

"There's nowhere else to climb!" he said.

Emily looked down. Frank was climbing up after them.

Jacob's long scarf snagged on a branch.

"Stupid thing," Jacob complained. "I should have left it in the park."

Emily had an idea. "Here," she said, "give it to me."

Jacob took off the scarf and passed it over.

"What are you going to do?" he asked.

"This!" said Emily.

She looped the scarf over a branch and jumped out of the tree!

CHAPTER 6 Queen of the Swingers

Emily swung on the scarf like a monkey on a vine.

She jumped onto the Totem Pole's head and pulled the scarf free.

"What are you doing?" the Totem Pole yelled. "Get off me!"

"Stay still," Emily said. "I've got a present for you!"

On the tree, Frank the monster had nearly reached Jacob.

"Hey, Frank old pal!" Jacob said, nervously. "You don't want to eat me! I'll taste horrible!"

He looked over at Emily.

She was busy stuffing one end of his scarf into the Totem Pole's ear.

"Hee-hee!" the Totem Pole giggled. "That tickles."

Emily looped the scarf over the Totem Pole's head and did the same with the other end.

"There," she said. "How does that feel?"

"Pardon?" the Totem Pole said. "I can't hear a thing."

Emily smiled. "Exactly," she said. "Now you'll be able to get some sleep."

"Hey," the Totem Pole said. "Now I'll be able to get some sleep!"

"So why don't you call off your monsters!" Jacob yelled from the top of the tree.

"I suppose I should call off my monsters," the Totem Pole said and blinked its eyes.

All over the jungle, the monsters shrank back down to normal size. The lion was running away from a small mouse. The gorilla was wrestling a tiny ladybird.

And Frank was a hamster again!

A hamster that suddenly found himself at the top of a very tall tree.

"Waaaah!" he squealed. "I can't stand heights!"

"Don't worry," said Jacob. "I'll get you down."

He carried Frank to the bottom of the tree.

"What happened to the Totem Pole?" Frank asked.

"Shhhh," Emily said, putting her finger to her lips. "It's asleep."

Sure enough, the Totem Pole had closed its eyes and was snoring loudly.

"And it said everyone else was noisy!" Frank laughed, before his eyes went wide.

He was staring at Jacob.

Something was sat on Jacob's shoulder!

Something with a lot of legs!

"Help!" Frank screamed. "It's a hamster-eating spider!"

With that, Frank ran all the way back to Adventure Park.

Emily looked at Jacob's shoulder and giggled.

It was just a bunch of bananas.

"They were growing in the tree," Jacob grinned. "Don't worry. I'll let Frank have one when he's calmed down."

Questions

1. What did Albert bounce into? (*page 8*)
2. Where did he get the seeds for the rainforest? (*page 12*)
3. What was chasing the lion? (*page 17*)
4. Why was the Totem Pole turning animals into monsters? (*pages 19–20*)
5. What did Emily do with Jacob's scarf? (*page 26*)
6. What did Frank think was on Jacob's shoulder? (*page 28*)

SUPER SPACE ELEVATOR
JOUSTING DODGEMS
DINO DANGER
GHOST TRAIN
PIRATE SHIP
GIFTS
RIP
PYRAMID MAZE
RAINFOREST RIOT
RAINBOW ROLLER
ADVENTURE PARK

Cavan Scott spends his days making up stuff – and he loves it! He's written for *Star Wars, Doctor Who, Adventure Time, Skylanders, Angry Birds, Penguins of Madagascar* and *The Beano*! He lives in Bristol with his wife, daughters and an inflatable Dalek called Desmond!

Meet the Illustrator

Abby Ryder is a cartoonist who loves comic books and video games. Her greatest life ambition is to one day become best friends with a giant robot.